CVEP

Published by Calithumpian Press, LLC
CalithumpianPress.com

Book designed by Paul Williams and edited by Lisa Pliscou.

The text in this book is Neutraface by House Industries. The font for the title is Elroy.

A note about the art: We've made a few changes to the ceiling of the Sistine Chapel.
First, to make it easier for young readers to spot the famous *The Creation of Adam*
fresco, we switched its position on the ceiling with the "Adam and Eve" fresco.
Second, understanding that families differ on how they introduce nudity in art
to their children, we've utilized fig leaves as needed throughout the ceiling's
artwork. For an amazing virtual-experience of viewing the original ceiling, you
can visit:

http://www.vatican.va/various/cappelle/sistina_vr/

The Vespa name is a registered trademark of Piaggio & Co. SpA. Use of
the product name does not imply any affiliation with or endorsement by
the company.

First Edition – 2013

Library of Congress Control Number: 2013918871
Cataloging-In-Publication Data available

ISBN: 978-0-9886341-1-4

Printed in the United States of America
by Lehigh Phoenix, Hagerstown, Maryland.

10 9 8 7 6 5 4 3 2 1 ... up, up, and away!

www.KeeKeesBigAdventures.com
Facebook: KeeKee's Big Adventures
Twitter: @KeeKeeAdventure

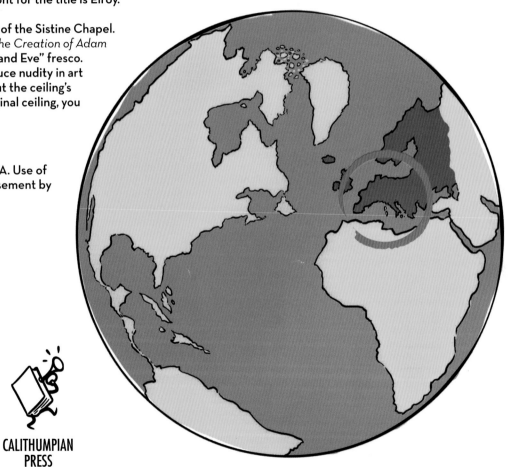

CALITHUMPIAN
PRESS

To all the kind, generous people and places
who take care of and find loving homes
for the world's furry friends,
including the Roman Cat Sanctuary
and the Seattle Humane Society,
where the real KeeKee was adopted.
Thank you!

KeeKee's Big Adventures
in Rome, Italy

Story by Shannon Jones
Illustrations by Casey Uhelski

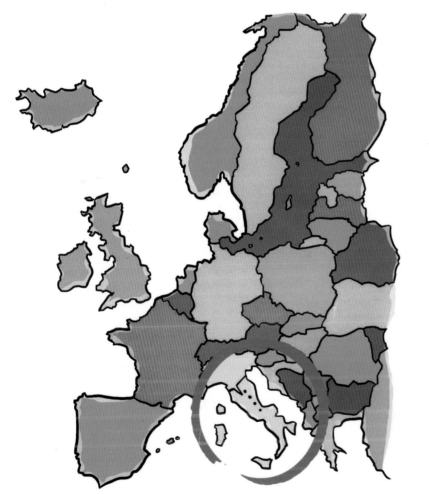

ROME

"*Benvenuto, Signorina!*" said Emilia.
"Welcome to Rome — the Eternal City!"

"*Grazie!*" said KeeKee. "I see I've landed in the PURRfect place!"

"Is this a shelter for homeless kitties and cats?" KeeKee asked.

"*Si, si,*" answered Emilia. "This is the world-famous Cat Sanctuary!"

"*Mamma mia!* I came from a shelter, too!" KeeKee said.

"What brings you to Italy's beautiful capital city?" Emilia asked.

"Well," KeeKee answered, "I've always wanted to..."

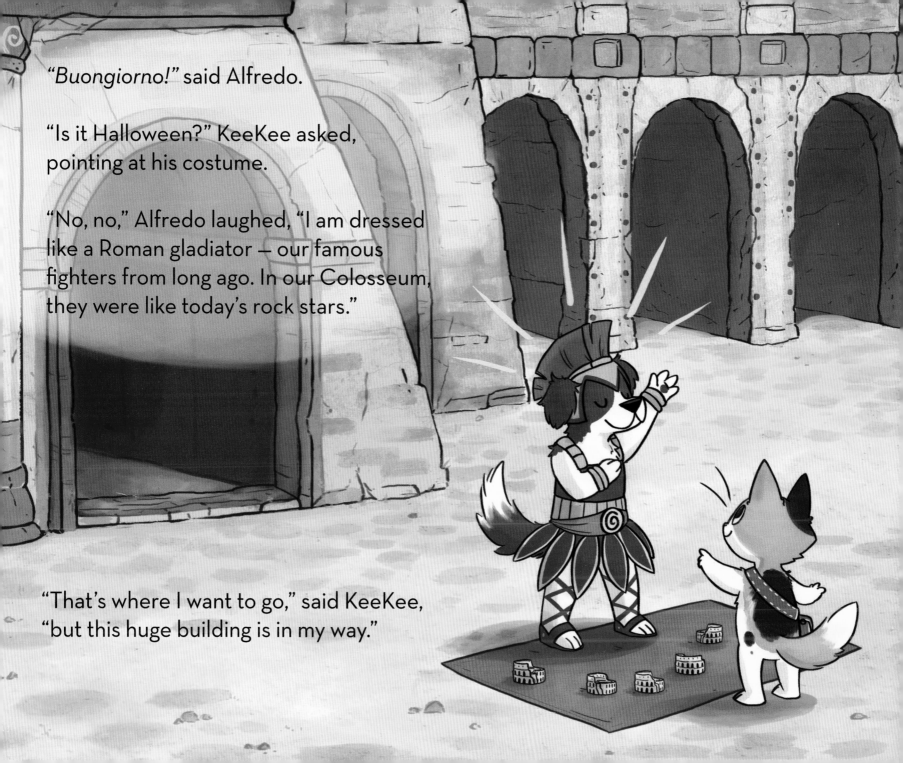

"*Buongiorno!*" said Alfredo.

"Is it Halloween?" KeeKee asked, pointing at his costume.

"No, no," Alfredo laughed, "I am dressed like a Roman gladiator — our famous fighters from long ago. In our Colosseum, they were like today's rock stars."

"That's where I want to go," said KeeKee, "but this huge building is in my way."

"This IS the Colosseum," Alfredo said.
"The biggest theater ever built."

"Big? It's **colossal**!" said KeeKee.

Alfredo offered to show KeeKee around.

whoa!

First, he led her to the Forum. "This was once the center of the great Roman Empire," he told her. "Speeches, elections, parades — it all happened right here."

"And now it's like a giant outdoor museum," said KeeKee.

"Back then, gladiators rode in horse-drawn chariots," said Alfredo, "but today, many of us Romans ride on Vespas to get around our busy city."

They zipped across town on Alfredo's modern-day chariot.

VRRmmmm...

"It's the Pantheon!" exclaimed KeeKee.

"The outside is amazing, but wait till you see the *inside*," said Alfredo.

"And now," Alfredo said, "I'm going to show you something *very* unusual."

"This is the *Bocca della Verità* — the Mouth of Truth," said Alfredo. "Some believe it will bite the hand of anyone not telling the truth."

"Careful!" said KeeKee.

As the afternoon sun heated up the city, KeeKee started to sizzle.

"That pool looks refreshing!" she thought.

sploosh!

plip plip

bonk

"When we Romans want to cool down, we go for a frozen treat, a *gelato* or a *granita* with cream," said Alfredo. "We call this enjoying *la dolce vita* – the sweet life."

MVSEI VATICANI

KeeKee had one more item on her list.

"Finally, the Sixteenth Chapel," she said. "Where are the other fifteen?"

"It's the *Sistine* Chapel," said Alfredo.

"Ohhhhhhhh," said KeeKee.

Cappella Sistina

"Splendido!"
said KeeKee.

She could see why
it took the amazing
artist Michelangelo
four years to paint
the ceiling.

"When in *Roma*, you must eat pizza,"
said Alfredo. "Peppe's is my favorite."

"Peppe's Pizza on the *piazza* is
perfect," giggled KeeKee.

"*Ciao*, Peppe!" Alfredo said. "This is *amico mio* KeeKee. She wants to try your pizza."

"Yes, I'd like 23 pizzas with extra cheese, please," said KeeKee, "and extra *extra* anchovies!"

"You must be very hungry!" said Peppe.

"I sure am," KeeKee said with a smile. "Oh, and can you make them to go?"

"Careful, Alfredo!" shouted KeeKee. "I've got the Leaning Tower of Pizza back here!"

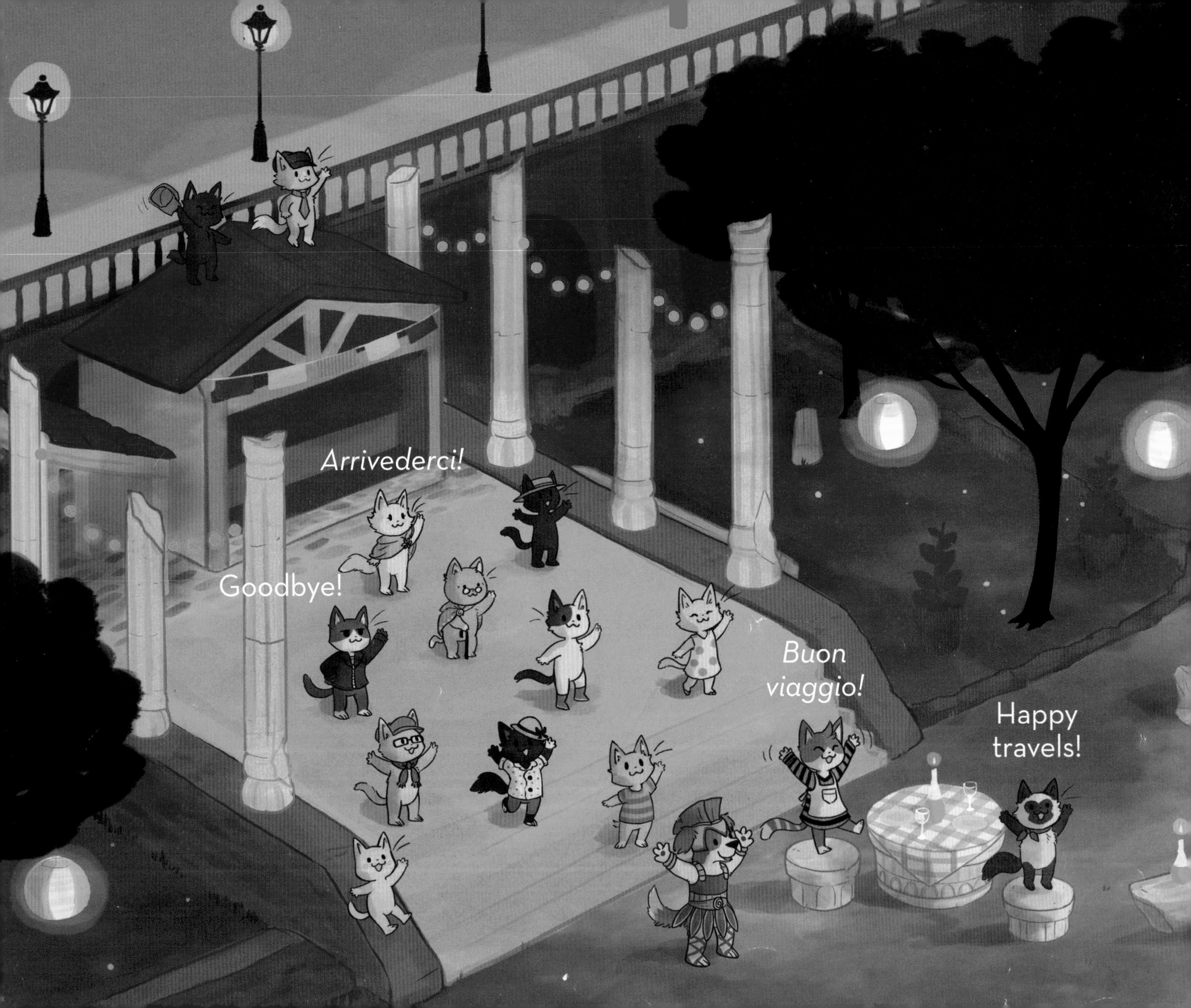
Arrivederci!
Goodbye!
Buon viaggio!
Happy travels!

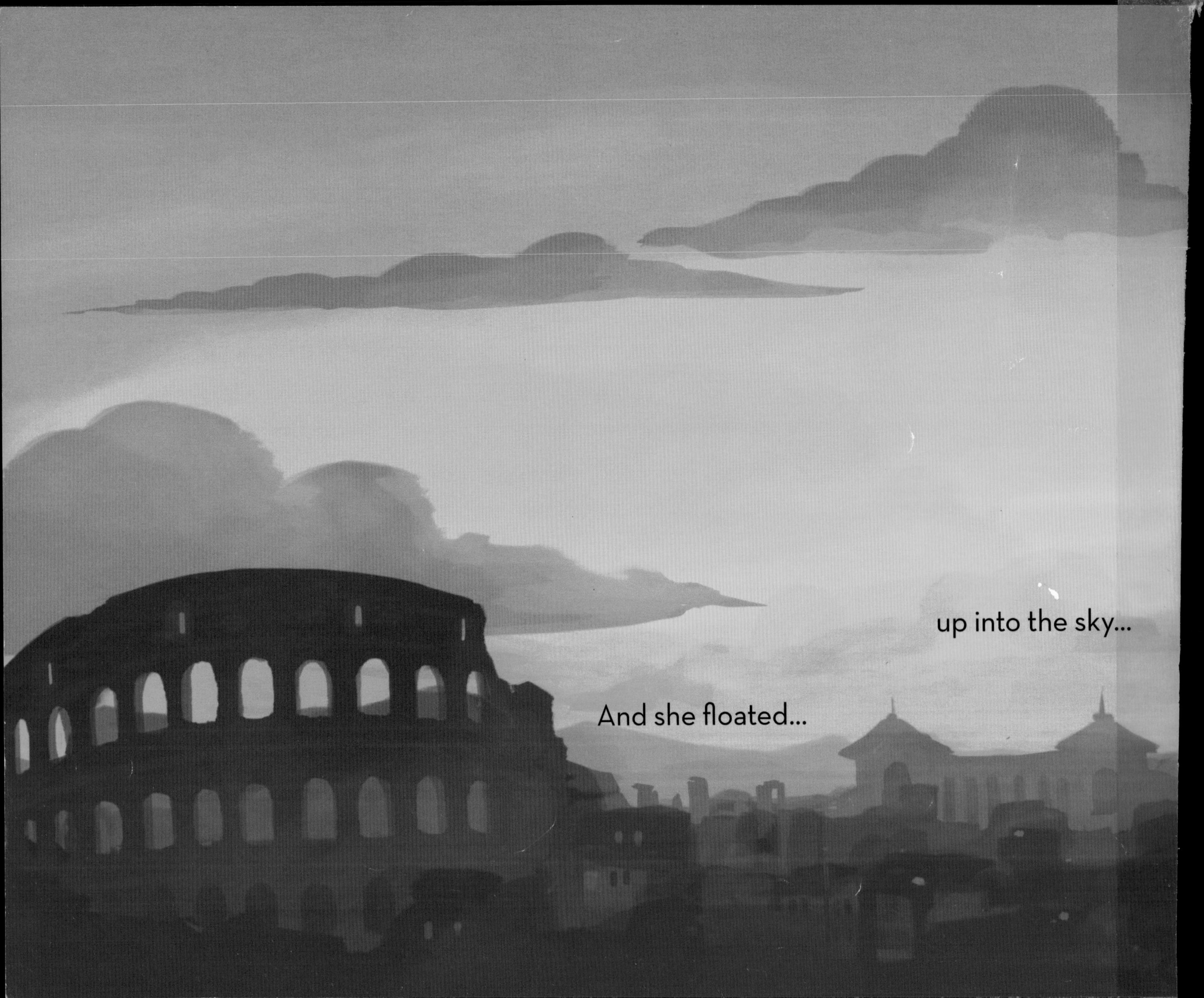

up into the sky...

And she floated...

Pronunciation Guide & Glossary

Words & Phrases

Amico mio	(ah-MEE-coe MEE-oh)	My friend
Arrivederci	(ah-ree-veh-DARE-chee)	Goodbye
Benvenuto	(ben-veh-NOO-toe)	Welcome
Buon appetito	(bwohn ah-peh-TEE-toe)	Enjoy your meal
Buon viaggio	(bwohn vee-AH-joe)	Happy travels
Buongiorno	(bwohn JOR-noe)	Hello
Ciao	(chow)	Hello / goodbye
Gelato	(jeh-LAH-toe)	Ice cream
Granita	(grah-NEE-tah)	Flavored ice
Grazie	(GRAHT-see-eh)	Thank you
Grazie mille	(GRAHT-see-eh MEE-leh)	A thousand thanks
La dolce vita	(lah DOHL-che VEE-ta)	The sweet life
Mangia	(MANH-juh)	Eat
Miao	(MEE-yow)	Meow
Mamma mia	(MAH-mah MEE-ah)	My goodness
Piazza	(pee-YAHT-sah)	Town square
Prego	(PREH-go)	You're welcome
Roma	(ROH-mah)	Rome
Saluté	(sah-LOO-tay)	To your health
Si	(see)	Yes
Signorina	(sin-your-EEN-ah)	Miss
Splendido	(SPLEN-dee-doe)	Splendid

Places

Torre Argentina Cat Sanctuary – This famous shelter is located among some of the oldest ruins in Rome. Volunteers feed and care for up to 300 feline friends.

Colosseum – The largest amphitheater in the world. It was once a venue for shows and games and held up to 80,000 people.

Roman Forum – This area was once the city's civic center. Today it is a mass of ruins.

Pantheon – Rome's best preserved building, dating back to the year 126. The huge hole, or oculus, at the top of the dome lights the entire building.

Bocca della Verità (BOH-kah deh-lah vehr-EAT-tah) – *The Mouth of Truth* is a large marble statue that used to be a drain cover. Starting in the Middle Ages, some believed that if a person told a lie with their hand in the Mouth, it would be bitten off. Chomp!

Trevi Fountain – One of the world's most famous fountains. (Unfortunately, no swimming is allowed.) According to legend, using your right hand to toss a coin over your left shoulder will guarantee a return visit to Rome.

Spanish Steps – A beautiful old staircase featuring 135 steps, the widest in Europe. It's a popular spot to drink in *la dolce vita.*

Sistine Chapel – Located in the Vatican Museums, the Chapel ceiling has 366 figures painted by the famous artist Michelangelo over four years and finished in 1541.

Piazza Navona (pee-YAHT-sah nah-VOH-nah) – One of Rome's most famous squares, it features many cafés, fountains with marble statues, and an Egyptian obelisk.